Dear Parents:

Congratulations! Your child is taking the first steps on an exciting journey. The destination? Independent reading!

STEP INTO READING® will help your child get there. The program offers five steps to reading success. Each step includes fun stories and colorful art or photographs. In addition to original fiction and books with favorite characters, there are Step into Reading Non-Fiction Readers, Phonics Readers and Boxed Sets, Sticker Readers, and Comic Readers—a complete literacy program with something to interest every child.

Learning to Read, Step by Step!

Ready to Read Preschool–Kindergarten
• big type and easy words • rhyme and rhythm • picture clues
For children who know the alphabet and are eager to begin reading.

Reading with Help Preschool–Grade 1
• basic vocabulary • short sentences • simple stories
For children who recognize familiar words and sound out new words with help.

Reading on Your Own   Grades 1–3
• engaging characters • easy-to-follow plots • popular topics
For children who are ready to read on their own.

Reading Paragraphs   Grades 2–3
• challenging vocabulary • short paragraphs • exciting stories
For newly independent readers who read simple sentences with confidence.

Ready for Chapters   Grades 2–4
• chapters • longer paragraphs • full-color art
For children who want to take the plunge into chapter books but still like colorful pictures.

STEP INTO READING® is designed to g reading experience. The grade levels are through the steps at their own speed, dev

Remember, a lifetime love of reading start

Visit us on the Web!
StepIntoReading.com
randomhouse.com/kids

Educators and librarians, for a variety of teaching tools, visit us at
RHTeachersLibrarians.com

ISBN 978-0-385-37503-0 (trade) — ISBN 978-0-385-37504-7 (lib. bdg.)

Printed in the United States of America
10 9 8 7 6 5 4 3 2 1

nickelodeon

DORA the explorer

Fairytale Magic!

By Kristen L. Depken

Illustrated by Victoria Miller

Random House 🏠 New York

The king and queen

of Fairytale Land

need help.

Their rainbow vine
needs magic water.
Fairytale Land will lose
its magic without it.
Dora and Boots will help!

The king gives Dora
some magic tools:
a brush, a music box, a ring,
and a bag of sunshine.

Dora checks Map.
Dora and Boots go
into a dark forest.

The Big Bad Wolf blows

Dora and Boots

up into the trees!

How will they get down?

Dora checks Backpack.

The magic brush!

<u>Brush, brush!</u>

Dora's hair grows

long and strong.

It helps Dora and Boots
get past
the Big Bad Wolf.

11

Soon Dora and Boots
find a giant's cave.
Their friends
are trapped inside!

Dancing will
open the cave.
Dora uses the music box.
She and Boots dance.
Their friends are free!

Next, Dora and Boots

find dragon flowers.

A spell has turned them

into snappy dragons!

Dora uses the magic ring.

It breaks the spell.

The flowers stop snapping.

Dora and Boots can go!

Dora and Boots
find a sparkly lake.
It is full
of magic water!

They take a boat
to the center.
They use a magic pitcher
to collect some magic water.

Oh, no—a witch!
She makes storm clouds
to stop Dora and Boots.

The bag of sunshine!
Dora uses it
to chase away
the clouds
and the witch.

Dora fills
the magic pitcher.
A rainbow appears!
A unicorn comes down
from the sky.

The unicorn takes
Dora and Boots
to the rainbow vine.

Dora and Boots
get there just in time!
They use the magic pitcher
to water the rainbow vine.

The vine begins
to grow.
Fairytale Land is saved!

Thanks to Dora and Boots, Fairytale Land will have magic forever!